Mag the Magnificent

Dick Gackenbach

Clarion Books
TICKNOR & FIELDS/NEW YORK

Clarion Books
Ticknor & Fields, A Houghton Mifflin Company
Copyright © 1985 by Dick Gackenbach

Printed in the U.S.A.

Library of Congress Cataloging in Publication Data
Gackenbach, Dick.
Mag the magnificent.
Summary: A boy's drawing on the wall of a magical
monster sets off a series of adventures for the two of
them, until his mother wants the wall cleaned off.
1. Children's stories, American. [1. Drawing—
Fiction. 2. Magic—Fiction. 3. Monsters—Fiction]
I. Title.
PZ7.G117Mag 1985 [E] 85-2645
ISBN 0-89919-339-0

Y 10 9 8 7 6 5 4 3 2 1

This book is dedicated to Carol Goldenberg

When I wear my Indian suit, magical things always happen.

One day, I put on my buckskin top. Then I put on my buckskin pants. By the time I put on my moccasins, the magic began.

"Draw me," I heard a voice say. "Draw me on your wall!"

Good magic guided my crayon as I drew.

I drew two bulging eyes and a great big nose.

I drew a good set of teeth, and two curly horns.

I drew little tin bells on his legs.

The monster was magnificent!

I decided to call him Mag, for short.

Then I did a war dance until everything turned rosy and Mag came off the wall to play with me.

Anything can happen when I wear my Indian suit!

Mag and I read books
and played games together.
We rumped and jumped and
made a mess of my room.

After that, Mag and I went to a supermarket.
A supermarket full of asparagus.

"I hate asparagus!" I told Mag.

As a favor to me, Mag ate all the
asparagus.

"Thanks," I said. "Now I'll never have
to eat another one."

It's neat to have a friend like Mag.

Then Mag and I took a walk to look for "don't" signs. There are "don't" signs everywhere. I hate "don't" signs even more than I hate asparagus.

As a favor to me, Mag made all the "don't" signs disappear.

It's great to have a friend like Mag.

I was glad Mag was with me when I
met Eleanor Osborne.

"She always picks on me," I told Mag.

"Eleanor Osborne twists my arm and
pushes me around!"

As a favor to me, Mag changed
Eleanor Osborne into a big fat old moose.
Boy! It's something to have a friend
like Mag.

Whatever I wanted, Mag could do. He could make it snow on a summer day, or fill a room with giant leaping frogs.

Mag could even turn things into chocolate candy.

Everything was going great until I
heard my mother's voice.

"TAKE OFF THE INDIAN SUIT. AND PLEASE
WASH THAT THING OFF THE WALL."

I knew my mother meant it. She left
me a pail of soapy water and a rag. Mag
would have to go, no doubt about it.

I did what I was told. But as I
washed Mag from the wall, I whispered,
"Don't worry, Mag, I have a plan!"

When my wall was clean and no one was looking, I drew Mag behind my mirror.

I drew him very, very small.

Mirror, mirror, on my wall,
Guard magic Mag until I call.

Someday I'll wear my Indian suit again.